YASMIN

The Builder

written by
SAADIA FARUQI

illustrated by
HATEM ALY

PICTURE WINDOW BOOKS
a capstone imprint

To Mariam for inspiring me, and
Mubashir for helping me find the
right words —S.F.

To my sister, Eman, and her amazing
girls, Jana and Kenzi —H.A.

Yasmin is published by Picture Window Books,
a Capstone Imprint
1710 Roe Crest Drive
North Mankato, Minnesota 56003
www.mycapstone.com

Text © 2019 Saadia Faruqi
Illustrations © 2019 Picture Window Books

Library of Congress Cataloging-in-Publication Data
Names: Faruqi, Saadia, author. | Aly, Hatem, illustrator. Title: Yasmin the builder /
by Saadia Faruqi ; illustrated by Hatem Aly. Description: North Mankato, Minnesota
: Picture Window Books, [2018] | Series: Yasmin | Summary: As their makerspace
project the students in Yasmin's second grade class are building a city: there are
houses, a school, a church, even a castle, but Yasmin is not sure what to build--
until inspiration strikes. Identifiers: LCCN 2017060504 (print) | LCCN 2017061833
(ebook) | ISBN 9781515827344 (ebook PDF) | ISBN 9781515827276 (hardcover) |
ISBN 9781515827306 (pbk.) Subjects: LCSH: Muslim girls--Juvenile fiction. | Pakistani
Americans--Juvenile fiction. | Makerspaces--Juvenile fiction. | Creative ability--Juvenile
fiction. | Elementary schools--Juvenile fiction. | CYAC: Creative ability--Fiction. |
Building--Fiction. | Schools--Fiction. | Muslims--United States--Fiction. | Pakistani
Americans--Fiction. Classification: LCC PZ7.1.F373 (ebook) | LCC PZ7.1.F373 Yas 2018
(print) | DDC [E]--dc23 LC record available at https://lccn.loc.gov/2017060504

Editor: Kristen Mohn
Designer: Aruna Rangarajan

Design Elements:
Shutterstock: Art and Fashion

Printed and bound in the United States of America.
060619 002230

TABLE OF CONTENTS

CHAPTER 1

A New Project

Ms. Alex walked into class with a big box.

"We are going to build a city today!" she announced.

The students were very curious. They all crowded around Ms. Alex as she opened the box.

There were tubes and tape,

long sticks and round wheels.

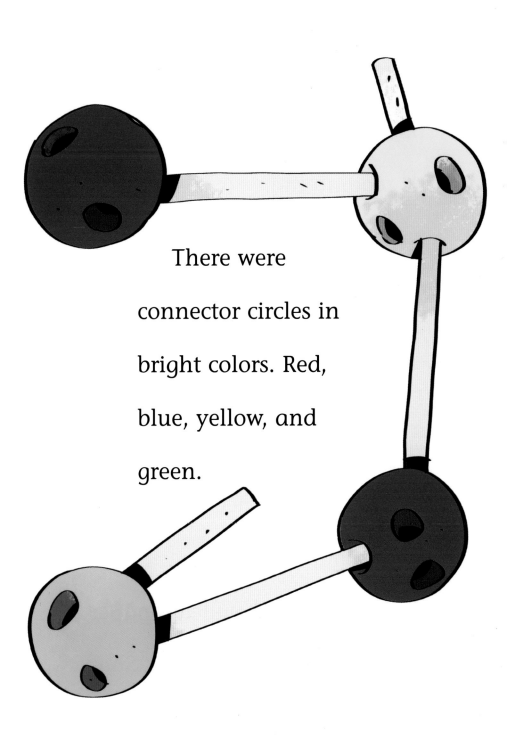

There were
connector circles in
bright colors. Red,
blue, yellow, and
green.

Yasmin watched as Ms. Alex spread the building parts all over the reading rug.

"When can we start?" Ali asked. He reached for a long stick.

"Not yet," replied Ms. Alex. "First you will draw your idea on paper. That way you'll know what supplies you will need."

"Boring!" said Ali.

Yasmin slowly pulled a paper from her desk. She doodled. She sketched. She sighed.

How would these pieces on the floor turn into a city? She didn't know what to make. A roller coaster? An apartment? A zoo?

CHAPTER 2

Get Ready to Build

Finally, Ms. Alex told the students to begin their buildings. "Think of everything a city has," she said. "Be creative!"

Ali was quick. In a few minutes, he built a castle.

"A castle in a city! I wish I'd thought of that," Yasmin said.

Emma was slower. Her church was very tall and had a pointy steeple. "Now I need to make some people," Emma said.

Yasmin sat in the corner, watching the others. She chewed her lip. This was harder than she'd thought.

"Yasmin, why aren't you building something?" Ms. Alex asked.

"All the good ideas are already taken," Yasmin said.

"Well, what do you like to do best in the city?" Ms. Alex replied.

Yasmin shrugged. "I like to take walks. But you don't need to build anything for that."

Slowly Yasmin joined two long sticks together. Then two more. She had no idea what she was making. At least she looked busy.

CRASH!

Yasmin's stick tower fell down into a pile. She hid her face in her hands. What a mess.

CHAPTER 3

Connecting the Dots

Soon, the bell rang for recess.

"We can finish after we get back," said Ms. Alex.

The students left, but Yasmin stayed behind. In the quiet room, she stared at the buildings. There was Ali's castle and Emma's church.

There was a school and three houses. A tall building that looked like a hotel. A grocery store and a gas station and a movie theater.

And Yasmin's messy heap.

She could hear kids playing outside.

"We may go for a walk this afternoon," she heard Ms. Alex call out.

That gave Yasmin an idea. She got to work, collecting all the leftover blocks and sticks and cardboard. She joined them together, here and there.

The recess bell rang just as she finished. Everyone came back in.

Ms. Alex was surprised.

"Yasmin, what's this?"

Yasmin smiled proudly.

"The buildings were lonely.

I joined them together with

sidewalks and bridges."

"Now the people can take walks and visit each other!"

"Wonderful idea, Yasmin," said Ms. Alex.

Emma said, "Hurray for Yasmin the bridge builder!"

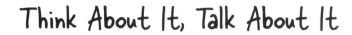

Think About It, Talk About It

* Yasmin has trouble coming up with an idea for the city her class is building. How do you come up with new ideas? What would you add to the city project if you could?

* What is your favorite thing about your city or neighborhood? What do you wish you could change?

* Think about a time you and a friend or classmate worked together on a project. Was it easier to come up with ideas when working with a partner?

Learn Urdu with Yasmin!

Yasmin's family speaks both English and Urdu. Urdu is a language from Pakistan. Maybe you already know some Urdu words!

baba (BAH-bah)—father

hijab (HEE-jahb)—scarf covering the hair

jaan (jahn)—life; a sweet nickname for a loved one

kameez (kuh-MEEZ)—long tunic or shirt

mama (MAH-mah)—mother

naan (nahn)—flatbread baked in the oven

nana (NAH-nah)—grandfather on mother's side

nani (NAH-nee)—grandmother on mother's side

salaam (sah-LAHM)—hello

sari (SAHR-ee)—dress worn by women in South Asia

Pakistan Fun Facts

Yasmin and her family are proud of their Pakistani culture. Yasmin loves to share facts about Pakistan!

Location

Pakistan is on the continent of Asia, with India on one side and Afghanistan on the other.

Capital

Islamabad is the capital, but Karachi is the largest city.

Sports

The most popular sport in Pakistan is a bat-and-ball game called cricket.

Nature

Pakistan is home to K2, the second highest mountain in the world.

Build a Castle with Yasmin and Ali!

SUPPLIES:

- shoebox
- construction paper of various colors
- scissors
- tape or glue
- markers
- empty oatmeal container, paper towel tubes, or other cardboard cylinders
- craft foam
- plastic straw or bamboo skewer

STEPS:

1. Wrap the shoebox with construction paper and tape it on. Draw on windows and a door. Set box upside down.

2. Cut paper to cover the assorted cardboard tubes/cylinders and tape on. Glue or tape them to the shoebox to make the castle towers.

3. Draw windows on the towers.

4. Make the roofs of the towers by cutting the craft foam into small cones and gluing them to the tops of the tubes.

5. Cut a flag from the construction paper and tape it to the straw or skewer. Glue your flagpole to a tower on your castle!

Saadia Faruqi is a Pakistani American
writer, interfaith activist, and cultural
sensitivity trainer previously profiled
in *O Magazine*. She is author of the
adult short-story collection, *Brick Walls:
Tales of Hope & Courage from Pakistan*.
Her essays have been published in
Huffington Post, *Upworthy*, and *NBC
Asian America*. She resides in Houston,
Texas, with her husband and children.

Hatem Aly is an Egyptian-born illustrator whose work has been featured in multiple publications worldwide. He currently lives in beautiful New Brunswick, Canada, with his wife, son, and more pets than people. When he is not dipping cookies in a cup of tea or staring at blank pieces of paper, he is usually drawing books. One of the books he illustrated is *The Inquisitor's Tale* by Adam Gidwitz, which won a Newbery Honor and other awards, despite Hatem's drawings of a farting dragon, a two-headed cat, and stinky cheese.

Join Yasmin
on all her adventures!

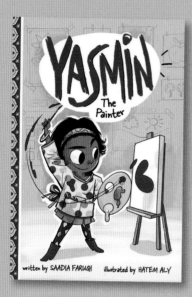

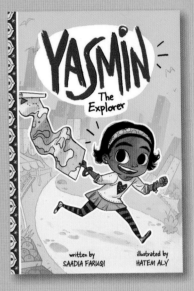

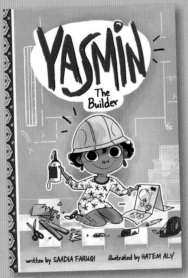

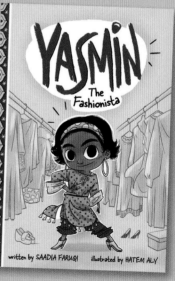

Discover more at
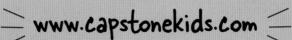
www.capstonekids.com